1994

To: Madison

Your 4th birthday

Happy Reading!

Couldn't help think of
you when I saw this
book!

Love,

Nana Kennedy

The Jewel Heart

BARBARA HELEN BERGER

Philomel Books · New York

Copyright © 1994 by Barbara Helen Berger

All rights reserved. This book, or parts thereof, may not be reproduced
in any form without permission in writing from the publisher.
Philomel Books, a division of The Putnam & Grosset Group,
200 Madison Avenue, New York, NY 10016.
Philomel Books, Reg. U.S. Pat. & Tm. Off.
Published simultaneously in Canada.
Printed in Hong Kong by South China Printing Co. (1988) Ltd.
The illustrations for this book were created using
acrylic paint and colored pencil.
Book design by Nanette Stevenson and Barbara Helen Berger.
The text is set in Goudy Old Style.

Cataloging-in-Publication data on file with
the Library of Congress and available upon request.

1   3   5   7   9   10   8   6   4   2

First Impression

To My Auntie Barbara

Gemino had a jewel for a heart.
But he had no voice.
He could sing only with his violin.

His song was for Pavelle.
When he drew the bow across the strings,

she danced.
And everyone whispered, "Ahh."

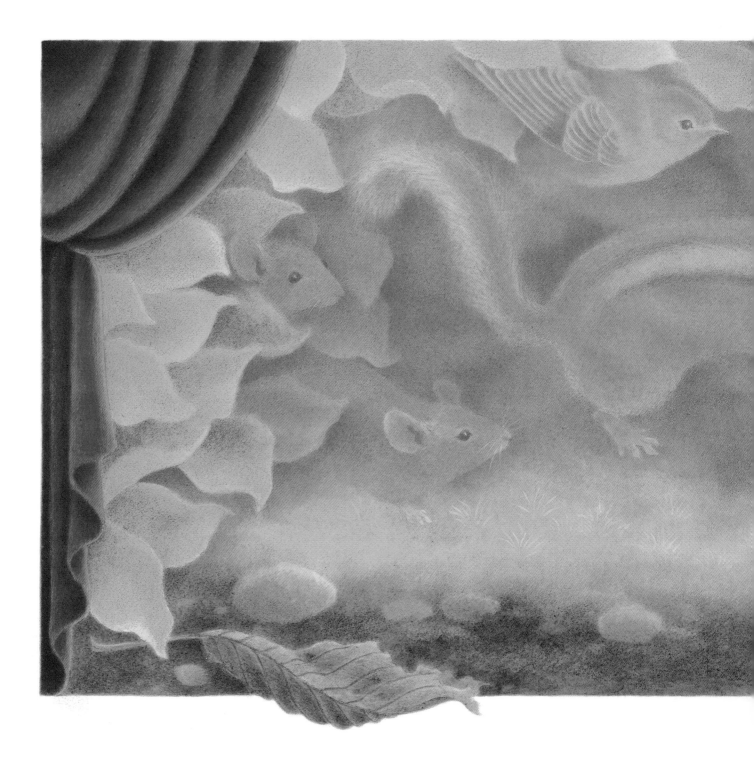

Then one day, Gemino was missing.
His violin was gone too.
Pavelle stamped her foot.

"How can I dance without a song?" she said.
"Where is he?"
"Ohh," sighed the shadows, "come with us."

"He was running to play for you,"
the shadows said.
"It was late."
"He fell and hit his head on a stone."
"Then he lay so still,
a woodrat came and nibbled his hair,
nibbled his clothes, and took
his jewel heart."

Gemino lay in tatters.
His face was a fallen moon.
"Ooohh," said Pavelle.
Then the shadows found his violin.
Not one string was broken.
But without Gemino, Pavelle
would never want to dance again.

The shadows whispered,
"Can you fix him?"
"He'll need a new heart," said Pavelle,
"and new hair, and new clothes....
Quick, bring me something to sew with!"
At that the shadows scattered.
Soon they came back with spider's thread,
a spine from a thistle,
dandelion down
and one brown seed.

"Ouch," said Pavelle
when she took the thistle needle.
She threaded it with spider web.
Then she took pieces and patches of shadow,
every tint and shade.
She sewed them all together
with tiny stitches.
She worked and worked and made a new suit
for Gemino.

Even the snail shadow wanted to help,
and his silver trail was sticky.
So with touches of silver,
Pavelle lay tufts of dandelion down
on Gemino's head.
Still he did not move.
Not even an eyelid fluttered.
"Something is missing,"
the shadows whispered.

Pavelle began to cry.
"He needs a new heart," she said,
"and I have no jewel."
There was only the one brown seed.
It was dull and plain.
Her tears fell on the seed
like drops of rain.
"This is all I have," she said.
Then she buried the seed
inside Gemino's chest,
and she sewed him up again.

Pavelle waited.

At last, Gemino opened his eyes.

He was splendid in his new suit of shadows.

His face was a rising moon.
When he saw Pavelle, he reached for his violin
and he played a new song.

All the shadows whispered, "Ahh."
They had never seen such dancing.
Pavelle turned to Gemino

and gave him a deep curtsy.
Just then, a tiny bud sprang from Gemino's heart.
The bud began to open.

And to Pavelle,
it was finer than any jewel.